# 15 MORE SPLASHES OF FICTION

## A Collection of Short Stories

### JOHN CORRAL

ISBN-13: 9798764855158
ISBN-10: 1477123456

Cover design by: Art Painter
Library of Congress Control Number: 2018675309
Printed in the United States of America

*For Tanya*

*Life is too short for a long story.*

--MARY WORTLEY MONTAGU

# CONTENTS

# PREFACE

This is a collection of 15 more fiction pieces, short to very short in length, but long on the truths of live, its dramas and dangers, and its randomness.  The only real thread that runs through them is their tightness and precision.  Yet plot and character develpment are not sacrificed in favor of compression and theme.  From the author of *15 Splashes of Fiction* comes another highly readable collection. Enjoy!

# OH MARGIE, MY PRECIOUS DARLING!

*A short piece about loss…*
*Profound loss that never ends.*

It happened again today, after church, when I was walking home thinking about what I might have for breakfast. I was passing Lawrence's Hardware on Sycamore and saw he had a new stock of Petunias on display —one of Margie's favorite blooms — and stopped to buy some.

A few minutes later, when I was standing in line, I remembered; Margie was not at home, she had passed away two years ago in March. Sometimes when I walk back things like that to the shelf, I feel such a throbbing headache that I can't see to walk.

It doesn't happen so much now as it did during my first year without her, but often enough. I should get used to it: No more Margie. No more buying two of everything at the grocer for dinner. No more two of us. When that dawns on me, I feel it like an ache.

And there is no Margie when I have a thought I want to share, or a movie that we could see, or a book to read, a trip to take. I haven't actually gone anywhere since she's passed, and probably never will again.

I still talk to her sometimes, as if she can hear me, but not that often now. We talked a lot back then, shared things, about what we read in the news, or what we had discussed with others on the phone. I miss sharing… A lot.

Sure, we'd argue, and say some bad things to each other, but we always made up. And she would be so sweet after being so mean. That was her way, and I loved her for it. I was no saint myself, but she loved me too.

Of course, I have my son and daughter-in-law, but it's not the same.

Nothing's the same without her.

Even at the end, the bad last few months, we grew closer together. She was not a burden, and I told her that.

Yet, I don't want to make it difficult for my son and his wife. Toward the end, Margie despised that she had become such a bother to others, to doctors and nurses, relatives and friends. But she was never a bother to me I would tell her, *never*, not even for one second.

I have my plans for when I am ready to go. Everything is set and waiting for me. It will be quick, without much in the way of discomfort, cost, or drama; a dignified end to a life.

But all that may be years or even decades in the future. Until then, Margie will go on being a part of my life. I have left her things as she had them. Her clothes still take up most of the closet space, and the number of drawers filled with her things is double mine. The spices and herbs that she used in her cooking are still in the pantry. All that is not going to change until I leave this house.

My son says the house is too big for me, and that I should sell it and get something smaller. I know that. But what he doesn't know is that I like it that way because I can shout in it sometimes, and hear the echos. Not that often, but when I hurt so much inside. That's when I yell out: *Oh, Margie, my precious darling! You still share this place with me! And you will until I see you again on the other side!*

# THE BEST LAWYER FOR BRAD

*A story about an attorney's
last chance for redemption,
in court and life.*

**B**rad Winston liked his lawyer instantly the first time he saw him. And Steve Reynolds was one of the best, an all-star like himself who had come to his house the day after Brad was released from the hospital, one of over a dozen lawyers who contacted him then. His parents wanted the inevitable parade of lawyers delayed until after their son got home.

Of course, they came because Brad had a multi-million dollar case. He had been a star running back in college, All-American for three straight years and was expected to go high in the NFL draft, but was rendered a quadriplegic from the car crash with a police cruiser.

Brad selected Steve on the spot because he seemed to have prepared for the meeting and knew all the details of the case far better than the others. He also seemed sympathetic and genuinely sincere in how he would devote himself to winning the case. And that was Steve's best trait as a lawyer, his immediate empathy with people, his ability to get a jury to like him, and thus his client and case, over the opponent.

Steve focused on Brad's eyes that day, not wanting to keep returning to the array of trophies, awards, and pictures on the wall that his parents devoted to their son's achievements. Centered on the wall was a larger-than-life picture of Brad, a blow-up of a Sport's Illustrated cover. That showed Brad with a football in his hands and a beaming smile as he crossed the goal line after evading a tackler, looking as if he knew his future was as inevitable as the touchdown.

That expected future contrasted with what Brad was like now: He had no right arm or right leg, both ended with stumps, and his entire body below his neck was paralyzed from a spinal cord break. And there was no smile on his face, slackened now from weight loss and the morphine drip that kept his pain down to a bearable amount.

Steve took pictures of Brad only in boxer shorts that day. Photos that showed the abrupt changes from the smiling football hero to what he was like after the police car slammed into him while on a high-speed chase; with dulled eyes and a dulled future, a body morphed into half its former size, wasted by the effects of six operations, the loss of his right arm and leg, and atrophy of his entire body from disuse. He wanted the jury to see Brad that way, emaciated and withered away, the effects of his injuries far more important than Brad's dignity.

Yet Brad was not blameless. He was driving that night with an elevated alcohol level just short of the legal limit. And an eye witness said Brad failed to yield when others did after hearing the police sirens. Later, at his deposition, that witness said Brad had a clear chance to avoid the crash if he'd only swerved. "He didn't, and that caused the crash, not the police officer who was on a high-speed chase, doing his duty, keeping the streets safe." And that was the position of the police union's attorneys representing the officer involved, the City Attorney that didn't want the city to pay a huge sum to Brad, and the press.

"It's not a slam-dunk case at all, no matter what you hear from other lawyers," Steve said to Brad, "and that's why the city hasn't offered anything to settle. The matter is going to court, and that's why you need a seasoned trial lawyer, not some guy who specializes in settlements and will get you only ten percent or less of what you should get." He then added, "Our chances are better than fifty-fifty, but it's going to be a battle, make no mistake about that."

What Steve hadn't told Brad was that his reputation as a successful litigator had come from his first twenty years practicing law and not the last five. He had not seen the inside of a courtroom since he left Emerson and Myers three years before. And that he lost the last two cases he tried there. He had made crucial errors, bonehead mistakes that even a rookie attorney would avoid, and that's why he was fired. And he also didn't tell Brad he had never represented a plaintiff before; all his prior cases were as a defense attorney. But Steve wanted this case more than anything.

"Well, did you sign him up?" Said Roger. Brad was sitting in his small, disorganized office shuffling through papers when Roger came in, first through the anteroom where no secretary had been for months, and then into Brad's office.

"I did," said Brad, "frickin' aye, I did!"

Roger put up his thumb up and said, "I knew you could do it!"

"Now you have to help me get the case prepped. I don't have a secretary anymore, and can't afford to hire anyone for now. Not for the paperwork, I can do that, but for research and witness prep... Paralegal stuff."

"Sure thing. I can do that. I let my bar membership lapse after I retired, but I don't need it for paralegal work."

"We're a team then! Just like the old days back at Emerson and Myers, where you taught me the ropes. What was that, twenty-five years ago now?"

"Sure, a team, like the old days. Except…"

Roger said the word and let it drift it out there between them, bare and alone, but infused with meaning.

"I know," said Steve, "I promised you, didn't I? Not a drop, *not one drop*."

The next year passed quickly. Steve had a few other legal matters that came his way, but nothing as important as Brad's case which he spent 90% of his time on. And he visited Brad every few weeks and got to know the young man personally. As he said to Roger, "The kid is really smart, and is reading everything I leave with him, stuffy legalize filings or not. He's even thinking of getting a law degree after his case is over. Imagine that?"

But without any major cases, there was no steady income. Overhead and trial prep, expert fees, and court costs had exceeded a quarter million on Brad's case, almost exhausting Steve's payout when he left Emerson and Myers. Everything was riding on Brad's case. If he won, it would be worth $10 million minimum, perhaps as much as $30 million, of which Steve would net a third of that. That's what drove Steve on, relentlessly, through the year. That and… Something else.

What that was, Steve could not identify. Was it regaining something he'd lost, atonement for what he'd done, or not done? That something nagged at him, and he couldn't pinpoint or stop it. And it worried him, dejected him at times.

And when his spirits were down, he'd call Roger who always said something positive. "You're a winner and a tiger in the courtroom. There's no one better at jury selection or cross-examination. Your openings are masterful, and your closings the best." On and on, and Steve believed them… Or wanted to.

What Steve didn't want to believe was that he would falter again, lose his confidence after a ruling against him, and go to pieces. Being too high on himself sometimes brought that result if something didn't pan out, hitting him in the stomach like a brutal punch to the gut. And there were so many opportunities for that to happen throughout the trial.

◆ ◆ ◆

It was the night before the start of the trial, and Steve felt the old anxieties building once again. He would have to keep sharp from the beginning to the end. He'll have only minutes, maybe seconds, to question a prospective juror to know whether they will go his way, or not.

Then the opening statement. A great one is needed to get the jury on Brad's side. With the evidence so equivocal, he'll need the jury from the start. Steve had been working on his opening almost from day one, and Roger called it one of the best he'd ever seen. Will Steve be able to sell it? He knew every word by heart. But what about the delivery? Can he sound honest, believable, and persuasive?

He called Roger for a pep talk. No answer. He tried again, and still no answer. *Damn!* Why doesn't he get an answering machine or a service like everyone else? He tried Roger's cell phone. No answer. He called a second time and left a message: "It's Steve —Call me as soon as you can."

Steve recalled the conversation he had with Roger days ago. One that occurred after Roger noticed the bottle of Jim Beam half empty in Steve's desk. Roger hadn't been in contact with him since.

"It's just a shot once or twice a day, to keep me steady, that's all." Said Steve.

"You sure about that? Remember how you were doing before you were let go at Evans? They had to settle a bunch of stuff because of you and your... *problem*." Said Roger.

"That was then, not now. I'm keeping it under control so that I can win. And when I win, it'll be the largest fee ever for a personal injury suit in the state."

"That's *if* you win. And if you don't, you'll eat all the expenses you've poured into it. And then where will you be?"

"I'll win, *I've got to* win," Steve said.

"I'll win, I'll win, *I'll win*," he repeated again and again to anyone who questioned him on his decision to pursue the case to trial, spending so much time and money on it instead of going for the sure settlement of $500,000 that the city finally offered.

Steve didn't know how convincing he was to others, but he had never convinced himself. He recalled how his stomach felt as though he had been sucker-punched there when he thought about it.

Steve thumbed through the contents of his litigation suitcase one last time, closed it and set it next to the evidence-filled boxes stacked between the easels. Early tomorrow his legal service would cart it all to the City Hall courtroom where he and defense counsel would pick a jury.

Steve turned off the light and closed his office door with shaking hands. He thought about returning and taking one more shot from the bottle of Jim Beam, just to steady himself, but resisted that temptation.

He continued to the reception area and through the outer door.

His leather soles slapped and echoed off the gleaming marble. The elevator doors opened. Quickly, he stepped in. The polished aluminum walls reflected his seamed face, milky-white from weeks of preparing late into the night. His knees were wobbly, and his insides felt even worse as he toddled into the lobby.

Then he was out on the street. He started walking to his apartment two blocks away. A fine mist was falling, puckering the silk of the blue tie his wife had given him for luck on the last case he tried and lost. Was that an omen? He had lost Janet the same day.

Steve looked to his left and saw his reflection in the clear glass of Murphy's Bar. He stopped and saw the scene unfold before him of when he came home and heard his wife on the phone, her bright laughter at odds with how he felt that day after the losing verdict. He lashed out at her, accused her of seeing other men, maybe even talking to a lover there on the phone. And then he hit her, repeatedly, and sent her to the hospital. Of course, he had been drinking and wasn't himself then. But there was no excuse for that, *ever*, Janet said, and they divorced soon after.

Steve continued looking at his reflection, at other scenes and experiences.

All the drinking that he did after his wife left him, and the loss of his next trial as well. After that, he lost his job with the firm he'd been with for twenty years. And with that reputation, no other firm would hire him. On his own, he muddled through existence as a court-appointed counsel and picked up cases from friends, or case hawkers for a fee. Hanging around hospitals and funeral homes was shameful, but necessary for him. It kept him in booze if nothing else.

Steve remembered all the drinking he did even in his heyday as a trial attorney, but he had kept it in check, for the most part anyway. And the reasons for it: he was an orphan who had been through the foster parent system, and who had been abused sexually by a relative leaving him with emotional scars that never went away.

"You have problems, but so do most people," Janet had said driving him to rehab the last year they were married. "And you drink to make them go away. It's like there's nothing more you want in life, but your drinking."

"I want you," he insisted. "I love you, and I need you."

"It's either me or the bottle because you can't have both."

"That's why I'm doing this. So we can be together."

"Don't! Don't go in there thinking you're doing this for me, or us. You do this for yourself and forget about me."

Steve remembered going through detox for the second time, and for the second time, it wasn't successful. Within two months he took another drink after a stressful day, and then another, and then a third, then a fourth… Going on that way, day after day, until it was his usual routine once again.

Steve remembered his last stint in rehab which came after he was arrested for drunk driving, and had to be bailed out by Roger. The pact they made, which was also ordered by the court, was that Steve would go to detox again —his last chance for that, instead of being referred to the bar for possible disbarment. He'd also have to undergo 40 hours of therapy and an equal number of hours of community service.

"I'm back, sober and renewed," he said to Roger, "and can take on the Brad Winston case. Piece of cake for me now."

Roger was skeptical and thought that wouldn't be a good idea. Roger was the only person who knew Steve was driving the car that was being chased by the police cruiser that crashed into Brad's car. That's why Steve knew the case so well, and why he wanted to win it so badly. For redemption, as well as for the money.

"I know I can do a better job than all the ambulance chasers out there... Much better," said Steve. "And I'll tell Brad and his parents about my involvement after the trial. Sure, it's skittering on the unethical, but it's not illegal or against the bar's rules of professional conduct.

"Your call on that," Roger said, "but you have to promise not to take one drink... *not a drop* until the case is over. Promise me that."

Steve had raised his right hand and swore that he wouldn't take another drink until then, and unquestionably believed that.

He lasted longer this time, going almost five months without a drink. Of course, one drink led to the next, and the next, and the next, with each swallow making it more possible to take another, and easing the regrets that might have been, until everything, fears, and anxieties, memories, and remorse, had melded into a dull stupor. There was safety there, and that's what he sought, at least for awhile.

Funny that it was this case that he sought to take on that caused his slide back from sobriety. He had taken it on to prove he wasn't a loser, for his self-esteem, and to make amends in some way for his part in Brad's accident.

He had come all this way back, but it was the pressure of the trial that now brought him back to his old habits. He had put so much on this case; it was about too many things, too pressure-packed and too important. That was what he realized when he wasn't drinking, when he was clear-eyed and sharp and lucid. When he drank, he didn't have to think about those things.

Steve had always been fearful of something, fearful when he lost his parents in a plane crash, when he was molested regularly by his uncle, and when he was arrested for shoplifting, vandalism, and for joyriding. He straightened himself out after his last arrest, fearful that he would enter the juvenile justice system, a sure path to a criminal future.

Steve used the fear to turn his life around. It focused him, sharpened him, and gave him the will to succeed. But it was too much sometimes. Smoking pot helped him through some of the rougher days. But it was illegal, and he could go to prison if caught smoking it.

Later, he found that drinking helped to ease his fears, and that became his crutch. At first, one or two drinks were enough; then more were needed. So what if he was going through a full bottle of Jim Beam a night by his second decade as a lawyer, he could straighten himself up in the morning. A cold shower would revive him, and plenty of mouth wash would mask his breath. Two or three aspirin eased his headaches, and raw eggs helped his stomach recover.

But, his appearance began to deteriorate, with puffy eyes and a grayish pall to his face. And there was nothing he could do about the lack of sharpness in how he handled himself in court, losing a step or two came with age, he told himself, even though he was only in his late thirties then.

The firm tolerated him because he was talented and won his cases, but drew the line at losing. After his second loss in a row, he was gone.

Steve was still outside Murphy's bar, looking at his reflection in the mirror. The mist had turned to drizzle, and then to rain. He looked to his left and eyed the handle of the door. Grasp it and pull and he would be back into his favorite bar. *Once inside there's no going back,* he thought to himself. *If you start drinking again, you've lost before you've even begun.*

The thought was cold enough to freeze his hand and almost stop his heart.

What was this case about anyway? Was it all about him: to prove he wasn't a loser? To make amends in some way for his part that night years ago when the police cruiser hit Brad's car? Wasn't it about that? That was when he went into rehab and stopped drinking. He had come all this way back; even taken on this case to prove it.

Funny, but it was the pressure of the trial that now brought him to the brink of falling off the wagon.

If not that, was it the love of Janet that he lost? She had been the best thing in his life, his biggest fan, and the champion he wanted to be when he was winning his trials. Was it to show Janet he'd turned his life around, done detox, completed all the therapy, taken on Brad's case and won? All so he could knock on her door and tell her: "I'm back, all the way back as a lawyer. Give me a chance to turn things around with you. Remember how it was then? We can get it back. All of it. I can make you happy again, and I know you will make me the happiest guy on earth."

Or was it something deeper, something he'd dealt with all his life? Fear. That sense of worry that petrified him from childhood; nameless, but powerful, ferocious and unrelenting. But fear of what? And did it matter?

What was it that Roger said about that? That it was good? Yeah, because it gave you the juice to win. So what if it gave you the sweats and the shakes? You just had to fight your way through. You could do that. You had before. You could again. You know you could make that happen. And be the best lawyer for your client!

His mouth was drier than it had ever been, and he ached for that first drink of Jim Beam. He could see his reflection in the glass with the neon sign for Samuel Adams Lager above. Desperation and defeat never became him. He turned and walked down the street.

The rain became a mist again. And the night was not as dark. From somewhere inside of him, a light came on. He tilted his head back and opened his mouth; the cold, clean mist fell onto his waiting tongue. It would not replace the Jim Beam --that craving would torment him still— but it did feel invigorating. He steps became livelier.

Steve looked out at the night sky and saw the courthouse in the distance where he would walk into the next day. It was a place he had been hundreds of times before representing clients. And he remembered one of his first cases there when he was an Assistant District Attorney and assigned his first felony, a rape case involving a prostitute.

The victim claimed she had been raped by a taxi driver who, after she got into the cab, took her to an alley, looked the doors, and threatened her with a knife. Then he reportedly sexually assaulted her for almost two hours, after which she was bruised and bleeding, and had to seek medical attention. The ER reported the incident to the police; the taxi driver was located and arrested. But the case was viewed as a loser because the taxi driver said it was consensual, payment for a cab ride.

Steve had taken on the case with fervor and determination, brought in three men who witnessed the victim walking away naked from the alley wrapped only in a newspaper. She was bruised, crying, and traumatized. Then he had evidence introduced that the driver could lock the door from the front and that a knife found at the scene had been purchased by the cab driver.

As it turned out, the cab driver was not convicted, after two jurors failed to find him guilty. Feeling defeated, Steve offered his sincerest apologies to the victim. But she wasn't upset, and instead hugged him and thanked him profusely for believing in her and for fighting as hard as he had.

Steve knew then why he had become a lawyer. To champion those who are victims, represent them when others won't, and to do everything he possibly could on their behalf. That was what had first inspired him to become a lawyer. And why he loved being a lawyer. He loved protecting people in a court of law. He loved the feeling of accomplishment that he got from helping others fight—win or lose.

Steve was restored now in youthful passion and ardent zeal of representing his client, for the client's sake, and not his own. He knew he was *the best lawyer for Brad*!

# HENRY'S HARDWARE

*Before Home Depot and Lowes,
there was Henry's Hardware*

You're working under the sink in the kitchen, and you need something, a part. Something that broke, or something you broke while trying to fix something else. You don't want to drive all the way to Home Depot; it's too far, it's too big, and you always buy something else besides what you came in for.

You'll go to the place a few blocks away, Henry's Hardware, and he might have it, though you hate going there because the place is disorganized, and Henry likes to talk so much. To everyone, always.

Henry is old, maybe ninety, and he smells.

He greets everyone by name as they walk in, smiles with yellowed teeth, and you dread it when there's no one else in the place because you know he's going to come over and try to help you with what you came in for, after telling you the latest joke he's heard.

It's always about a man going into a bar. Or maybe two men, a Polish guy and a German. Or two women, a prostitute and a nun. Maybe there's an animal with the man, an ape, or a giraffe. No matter, what doesn't change is that he puts his arm on your shoulder and gets too friendly, too close.

And his jokes aren't funny. They're long, interrupted by coughing most times, and, more often than not, make no sense. Maybe they're funny to him, but they're not funny to you if you have to stand there smelling him, and wasting time listening instead of working on your project.

And after telling his joke, he asks what you need. A gasket? Sure, this way. "Let's see if we can find it."

And that's a challenge because he throws all the gaskets into a basket and you have to search for the right one as if it's a puzzle piece for a 1000 piece jigsaw puzzle.

Why can't someone else come in so Henry can turn his attention to them? Maybe business is bad because he is so friendly to everyone, or he's friendly because business is so bad?

Nothing like the old days when he first bought the place. Back then, most days, flocks poured in. He had help then, one or two full-time employees, and several more part-timers on the weekends. No more. That was pre-Home Depot, Lowes, and Home Base.

This week you needed something quick, a part for the toilet that keeps running. Again, you didn't want to drive to Home Depot for that. You go to Henry's Hardware, and it's closed. Permanently, says the sign.

You feel strange. Is that relief that you're feeling, that you won't have to put up with Henry again? Or grief that a genuinely warm and friendly man has passed. He was the ultimate neighbor, good-natured, kind, and generous with his time and attention. Someone who you dreaded having to see and put up with, but now never to see again.

You ask at the dry cleaners a few stores away, and they confirm that Henry died, there at his hardware store, last Monday. There was no funeral because he had no living relatives.

Your drive to Home Deport is one of the longest you have ever taken.

# THE PARTING

*A breakup to a romance remembered
long after it occurred, with very
vivid and emotional memories.*

We parted as friends, at least that was something I did right. But everything else was wrong about my breakup with Vivian. Even our last kiss, though I still loved her then, was all wrong. I leaned in to give her a quick kiss on the cheek, and she turned her head and gave me a long, deep kiss instead. Then she pushed her hair away and put her cheek to my chest, wanting to be held. But I didn't respond to the kiss or her closeness.

"We're not suited for each other," I said, repeating what the counselor told us. "And never will be."

"But you said I was what you were looking for," she replied as she pulled back. "And I felt you were the one for me."

"We had some good times, but the bad ones…." I didn't want to be incriminating again, and so I left it there.

She searched my eyes for some hope that this would not be the end, but it was. And I would have remained with her if I felt there was some hope that things would work out between us. But

I didn't think so, not after what the counselor had said. So I took her hand in mine, pulled it up and kissed it, and then turned and walked away. I crossed the street and looked back at her, but she had turned, and all I could see was the back of her head.

I have returned to that street corner where we parted many times and each time I find myself wondering *what if* we never parted, and *what if* my future would have been with her.

One time a girl who reminded me of Vivian had her back towards me looking through a shop window. She had the same strawberry blonde hair, thick and full that reached below her shoulders. She pushed it back as she leaned toward the store window, the same as Vivian

I never saw that girl's face --I didn't want to because it might have dissolved the illusion that it might be Vivian. I knew it wasn't. Eventually, the girl met an older woman, and the two walked off while I stared at their backs until they disappeared around a corner.

In a thousand dreams since I have re-crossed the street and rushed to Vivian, embraced her, told her I was sorry, and never left her side again. But that has only been in dreams. In reality, Vivian turned and walked away from me, and I never saw her again after that late July day in 1986.

I have about six months, perhaps less according to the doctors. There is little pain now. That will change as the growth that will take my life becomes fierce and terrible. So maybe two to three good months left and then . . . Well, they tell me I will probably welcome my end when it comes.

The diagnosis was made some months ago, and since then, I have thought a great deal about Vivian. Facing death causes one to look backward with added perspective and clarity.

You think about what you could have done or should have done, as well as what you actually did. You see things plainly and with heightened detail --like that girl with the strawberry blonde hair. I noticed that the sleeve of her sweater on her right arm was pulled up inches higher than was the left, and she was wearing bright red nail polish. You see your life with the same clarity. Mine would have been far better, fuller, and more complete spent with the only woman I ever loved, Vivian.

# AN AMERICAN INDIAN IN THE COURT OF ST JAMES'S

*A salty satire based on a true story.*

I am not entirely full-blooded Apache, but probably more 'full-brooded' than any Indian I know. I can trace my ancestry back almost a hundred and fifty years, through five generations, and no non-Indian relative is known to me. Before then, an early trapper must have sneaked his way into the family tree because I have clear blue eyes, not exactly an Indian trait. (This last thing came up often when my parents were arguing, and always in connection with a "Paleface" postman or cable guy.)

My skin color though is rich mahogany and shimmers in the sun a deep rust red, living proof that there is such a thing as a "Redskin." And similar to Geronimo, probably the most famous Apache, I am from the Bedonkohe band of the Apache tribe. And I am also like him in appearance with high cheek bones, wide eyebrows, a bony jaw, and extremely straight black hair. But we differ since I doubt he ever got drunk and had a tattoo of the Grateful Dead skull and lightening bolt tattooed above his penis.

Put a feathered breastplate on me, a leather loincloth, and moccasins, and I would be the quintessential Indian sent by central casting to any Hollywood Western… As I was back in the Eighties. I am now in my late Fifties but can pass for early Forties. I can bench press my weight, run a 5k in under 20 minutes, and can hold my own in a bar fight —the last of which was only weeks ago, resulting from not holding my liquor, another Indian trait.

How I got to England as a part of the official US delegation to the wedding of Prince Harry to Meghan Markle is an interesting tale. Sit back, have a cup of tea, enjoy it with some fresh scones and gooseberry jam, and I will tell you about it.

First, more about me. I was raised on tribal land east of Albuquerque, New Mexico. Of course, that doesn't distinguish me much since most Apaches come from there. After all, it is virtually all reservation, clear to the Texas state-line.

I was smarter than most of my fellow tribesmen, so I moved away to go to college. Most of them stayed home —and subsequently got hired by one of the Indian casinos where they nominally worked and made a fortune. No, I got a football scholarship instead and went to Florida State. With my build and look, they thought I would make All-American easily, like Jim Thorpe. The trouble is, I could never hold on to the football, especially after being hit by guys that were almost twice my size.

But Florida State made the best of it, and made me their mascot, Chief Osceola, and had me ride around on a horse in full Seminole regalia, brandishing a burning spear. I did that for a few years, even after I stopped attending classes. Then one Saturday afternoon, I was presented with a gold and gemstone-encrusted spear to carry when we were playing Notre Dame. Keep it safe, I was told, it's worth a small fortune. I did just that: during a touchdown celebration, I circled the field, turned left at the exit, and made it safely out of the stadium. After that, I kept going until I crossed the state line; two days later, I was in Texas, and by the end of the fourth day, I was back on the reservation. The spear? I sold it to an Indian museum in Albuquerque for $12,500 —no questions asked.

What did Florida State do about it? Nothing. Can you imagine the negative publicity if they had sued their mascot over some Indian artifact that they probably stole from the Seminoles anyway?

Next Hollywood came calling. Or, I should say, Hollywood came to Apache country. There was a film being shot in the tribal area when I returned. I was still wearing that Indian getup and actually resembled Hollywood's version of Indians better than the Indians on the set and was hired on the spot. I was a natural and appeared in dozens of movies over the next ten years.

Then came the Nineties. Not too many Westerns made then. Sure, I got small parts in Dances with Wolves and Geronimo, plus one or two others, but I mostly stayed home, *on the reservation*, so to speak, collecting my casino dividend of $1120 a month. The 2000's? I don't remember much of what happened then, or up until about 2018. It seems I developed a hankering for Meth and rode that "trail of tears" for quite some time.

It was Lily Two Trees that got me back into faux Indian work. Or was it her sister, Mariam Double Tree, her twin? Anyway, it was one of the Trees who learned that Indians were being recruited to join a Wild West Show that was going to be put on in connection with the Royal Wedding in England. It promised to be good wages for six months minimum; half salary while in rehearsal, plus housing and meals while there.

Also, a draw was that American Indians were considered "noble savages" by the society women of St James's Court. ("Court of St James's" is what diplomats call the place where England receives ambassadors. Why? Fuck if I know. What I do know is that that there are true "Ladies in waiting" there, and they have the hots for the inscrutable, but screwable noble savage.)

A similar Wild West Show put on in the West End of London back some years ago had turned many of the "Ladies in waiting" into groupies eager to bed as many of the "savages" as possible.

I'd heard those stories and was eager to find out if they were true. One of the veterans of that West End show was Tom Peterson, who changed his Indian name from Brown Bear Diviner to Brown Beaver Diver. Legend has it that he "trapped" three beavers in one night. Could I outdo him? I did back in high school, and Apaches love a challenge.

I did have to break up with my live-in, Pricilla, a mixed breed of Apache and Navajo who taught at the Indian school after majoring in women's studies in college. Break up? It was more like I was thrown out, clothes and all, once I mentioned an interest in the Wild West Show. My promise to her as I was gathering up my things was to do my own women's studies and catalog them by muff color and size of breasts. Her retort was, "They only want you for your body." To which I replied, "Now that's equality I can live with."

A week later I was in rehearsals for the show in London —that is, New London, Connecticut, which must have been some cosmic joke to the organizers. They rented an abandoned industrial plant that hadn't been used for years, cheap no doubt, and set us up on makeshift cots on the production floor. There were about thirty of us, divided equally between cowboys and Indians, with the best places, the ones near the heaters, given to the blond and blued cowboys. What else is new?

And even among the Indians, there seemed to be a pecking order. The haughty Nez Perce got the best, next came the Mohawk and the Seneca, both from New York State, the Seminoles from Florida after that, and the lowly Apaches and Navaho from New Mexico got the worst. Yes, I did consider filing a discrimination suit, but settled for pissing on the clothes of all the others every chance I got. But I think someone found out I was doing that since, by the third day, I was assigned to feeding and cleaning up for the horses and buffalo in the stock area. I was going to ratchet up my retaliation to include food, but thought better of it since we all ate at the same chow line, and frankly, I doubt I could get the food any worse-tasting than it was already.

Rehearsals took three weeks: the cowboys learned how to ride hard, shoot straight, and look triumphant; and the Indians how to hoot and holler, how to fall off our horses without breaking our necks, and how to die properly. Our part of the show was the finale, with the preliminary acts consisting of a guy performing rope tricks on horseback, a marksmanship exhibition put on by "Annie Oakley," and a stagecoach saved from a buffalo stampede by "Buffalo Bill." What the audience didn't know was that all three were the same person, a former Olympic champion in the shot put named Michele, who went by the name Michael after the Olympics. 'Nuf said on that.

We finally got to London, the real London, on February 22, and saw our accommodations there. They were even worse than the ones in Connecticut. I read Oliver Twist back in high school and remembered how Charles Dickens described Oliver's workhouse. He could have been describing the hostel we boarded at, The Waterloo, which we called The Waterless. There was no heat, the water was only heated once a day for an hour and looked pale ginger on its best days. The exposed lights in each room were 15 watts and flickered more than gaslight. This was Oliver's workhouse!

OK, we didn't spend much time there for sure, and thus it was no great loss. And the nights we did spend at The Waterless were just a few hours to catch our breath from everything else going on. Did I mention the "Ladies in Waiting"? You bet they were there. Of course, most had been waiting for decades and were passed up again by us, but not all. Me? I met Eleanor soon after I arrived.

Before I introduce you to Eleanor, let me tell you about the Wild West Show. It was staged at a football stadium, Craven Cottage, located on the banks of Thames River. With a capacity of about 25,000, it's one of the smallest in London, and oldest, dating back to the 1890s —during Dicken's time, and it showed. We had to accommodate the football club that played there, Fulham FC, plus some national teams from other countries, and an occasional rugby league match.

And here I need to clear up some things up to those "blokes" who wrote nasty letters to the editor in The Times and especially The Daily Star, that it was "cock up" to have the Wild West Show at Craven Cottage. The show didn't make a "a bloody hell" out of the field, it was always the rugby matches that did that. And as for complaining that the horses and buffalo "opened bollocks and shit on the field," it was always the national teams from other countries that did that. The Wild West Show had some problems, but not those.

First of all, most of the time the Indians were stoned. The Mohawks convinced the organizers that using peyote was required as a part of their religion. Soon after the Senecas claimed Marijuana was part of their religious practices, and they had to "practice" that religious rite daily. When I tried to argue the same thing about my use of Meth, the organizers drew a line on that. But at least I was assured connections for other "religious" substances. The cowboys? Jack Daniel's was their ritual drink of choice.

But the thing that really put us back was that we kept losing horses. Yes, literally, losing them. Every few days or so a horse would end up missing. We never learned why. The clerk at the hostel told us horse meat is considered a delicacy in Kazakhstan, and their embassy was just down the street. You get the connection, kemosabe?

Replacing them was a problem since the horses the Indians used were Appaloosa, our traditional mounts. We brought only two extra with us and they were gone by the second week. After that, the show bought some from nearby farms, but those came with problems: one was horse that always kept looking around to see what was going on, and the other refused to ever get beyond a mild trot. We called them Spotter and Trotter.

Now back to Eleanor. I met her after the first show we did, the gala which introduced us to London, and the one attended by the

Royals. No, not *the* Royals, but some minor cousins. Anyway, there was a reception after the show at The Savoy near Trafalgar Square, and everyone associated with the show went in costume. And was that place ever hotsy-totsy! The room had a crystal chandelier that was huge, almost the size of that space ship in Close Encounters of the Third Kind. The men all wore tuxedos, and the women had on designer gowns. It was like the Oscars, only no red carpet, and without the phony acceptance speeches. Who the fuck thanks half the world for something they do?

Remember a couple of years ago when *La La Land* was announced as the winner of the best picture Oscar and the producers were in the middle of thanking at least a hundred people when someone interrupted and said they got the movie wrong, and it was *Moonlight* that actually won? So that crowd left the stage, and another crowd took their place. Did you notice that many of the same people were thanked again? Check it out and see. The Hollywood "tribe" is smaller than most Indian tribes.

Sorry, back to Eleanor.

Her first words to me were, "The Scots don't wear anything underneath, do you?"

My reply was obvious: "Want to find out?"

Less than ten minutes later, we were in her place two blocks away where Eleanor's long fingers found out that indeed Indians were like the Scots in *that* way.

We must have made an odd pair walking through London the way we were dressed, she in a long white satin gown and fur, and I in buckskin, quill breastplate, and feathered headdress. Yet when the doorman let us into her fancy building, he nodded to her with the kind of look that maybe her latest companion was not that unusual, or one of so many that it didn't matter.

I didn't learn much about Eleanor that evening. I remained silent, playing the role of the inscrutable Indian, while she seemed to welcome the lack of questions on my part. She said little more than what you might expect during our lovemaking session that went on for hours. Plus, her bedroom had mirrors on three sides, with the plate-glass window offering a reflection as well, and so wherever we could be seen. Believe me, that kept my attention.

Did I say what we did was lovemaking? That's wrong. There was not even the hint of soft caresses, loving words, or any kind of foreplay. She wanted to be taken forcefully and aggressively. And I accommodated her. Again, and again, and again. When I exploded inside of her the last time, around three in the morning, she said, "That's enough. You must leave now."

I felt the same way. It had been a long day for me, and an even longer night. But I was concerned that I had done something wrong, so I said, "You're not sore now, are you?"

Sure, poor choice of words.

She smiled and said, "Only in the best way," and rubbed her belly.

"How can I con—"

She put her fingers to her lips and said, "No questions. I know how to reach you, and I will, when I can."

And when did Eleanor reach for me again? It was just a few days later. She sent a telegram —yes, a telegram to the box-office that read: My car will pick you up 30 minutes after the show ends. Be at the stadium gate in performance attire.

That became our routine. After every third day or so, she had her car —A Bentley, by the way, pick me up and take me to her flat where I was respectfully recognized by the doorman and let in. Her apartment, what she called a flat, was in a building owned by her husband. "He has lots of them," she said when I asked if her husband knew about it. "He can't be bothered if I have my own." I didn't know if she was referring to the flat or to what she did in it, and whether he had his own place for similar flings.

Other questions about her husband usually resulted in her saying, "Let's not talk about that." Or, "He has his life, and I have mine."

The most I got from her was once when I asked what he might do if he found out about me was, "We have an understanding."

It was toward the end of our time together, since the show would end in days, that she became more open about her husband. Picking up a vase with cornflowers painted on it, she wistfully said, "He gave me this when he was courting me." Then she said, looking away, "He bought it off a pushcart, on a sunny day in Florence." Then she added, "I spotted cracks in it immediately, that day in fact." I didn't know if she was referring to the vase or their relationship.

"What does he do, your husband"? I asked.

"He is an Earl —that's what he does primarily in life, and also an occasional businessman and politician. He is very well known. He works in the government. But I'm not going to reveal who he is."

And I never did learn his name.

I last saw Eleanor at the airport just before I boarded my plane to go home. She said she wouldn't see me off, but she appeared at a distance while I was there with several others from the show. Even that far away, I could see that her eyes were red and sparkling as if she was crying. I gestured with my hands to see if she wanted me to come to her, and she signaled no. But she did put her hand to her lips and blew me a kiss. I blew one back at her. Just then I noticed two others in the show did the same thing… Or was that my imagination?

# TYING A KNOT
# THAT BINDS

*Lessons in life from one generation to another can flow in both directions.*

"Do you think she still likes to fish with him," her father said, "because she's almost 13 now."

"She says she does… At least for one more year of it anyway. Coming to his cabin, because he's almost gone mentally, if not physically," replied her mother.

Rachel was in the back seat, eyes closed, but listening. *Amazing what they said,* she thought, *when they didn't know she was awake.*

"This is probably the last year when she isn't into boys and all that, and with no Wi-Fi or phone, it is like stepping back in time."

"I just hope it's worth it to come all this way and put up with him for two weeks a year. He said he'd leave it to us. At least we can look forward to selling it when he's gone."

"Who else would he leave it to? He hasn't talked to his sister Meg for years, and he doesn't have close friends."

Rachel was already awake when her grandfather cracked the door and looked in on her.

"Ready to go get them trout?"

Her grandfather had whispered those words, but in a rasping, low tone that was louder than people talked normally. He was nearly deaf and talked as if everyone else was as well. He was dressed in a flannel shirt, a fishing vest, chest wader held up by suspenders, and a Brooklyn Dodgers baseball cap he purchased the year before they left for Los Angeles.

"Can we have breakfast first?"

"Only if you cook it. I had my coffee, and made sandwiches for later."

When Rachel entered the kitchen, it smelled of coffee, strong coffee, and there was nothing she hated more in the morning. She opened a window and breathed deeply. Better, she thought.

"Anyone else coming?"

"Do you want them to?"

"No... Just asking."

As Rachel got the pan and eggs out, she noticed all the food scraps that had not been cleaned off the stove. *His eyes are getting worse,* she thought. Her own eyes needed glasses, which her parents said they would get for her soon, after other bills would be taken care of. She found it ironic that her parents still asked for money from him though he had little to spare, just a small pension and this cabin.

After they had finished the scrambled eggs, she went back and cleaned up the stove. Now they were ready to go fishing. She and her grandfather went by the bedroom where her parents were still sleeping, and she could hear the faint snoring of each. The wine they brought with them was one bottle less after last night's drinking.

The sun was just breaking over the mountains to the East and lit up the dew on all the surfaces. Rachel and her grandfather walked slowly, she keeping in time with his labored steps, and watching him so that if he lost his balance again, she could catch him. He was a tall man, but had lost weight and walked with a stoop now, his back caving in forward like he was about to fall.

In his pictures as a young man, her grandfather looked so much different before he married her grandmother, raised his two children, and before the car accident that took his wife and hospitalized him for almost a month. He had a full head of dark hair then, was brash and handsome, and had the physique of a lumberjack. Now he looked skeletal and anemic. She had only known him as this old man and wondered if she would have liked him as much as a young man.

"Alex," her mother had said to her father in the car on the drive up, "do you really think this is his last year? I'm not coming up here again if it's not. You can make the trip, but not me. I just hope to hell it's worth it for us in the end."

"He's your father, not mine. I never liked the old guy, and he's never liked me. Called me too short, and an Indian. What was that all about anyway?"

"Just talk, because of your high cheekbones and a dark complexion."

"Italian ain't no Indian, and better than his Viking roots."

"Rachel takes after him, you know, more than she does you."

"In more ways than one."

She watched as her grandfather struggled to tie the tippet to the teaser of his line. His fingers were too long and bony, the backs of his hands mottled with spots. He couldn't see well enough to make a knot.

"Here, let me help, grandpa."

"Damn this line! Always gives me trouble now."

"Just tell me what you want me to do."

"You need to make a knot from the two strands. Cross the lines over each other… Yes, that's it… Twist the ends around the opposite length… And then pull the tips through the loop and secure it…. You got it!"

He then gave Rachel the rod. "OK, now cast it. Gracefully, in one motion. Yes, that's it, sweetie, that's it!"

He continued to talk to her as she cast her line over and over again. He told her fly-fishing was the most elegant thing anyone could do. "Aim for the breaks in the current, that's where the fish are. More to the left. Yes, that's it. Easy now, no rushing it. Slow, as if you got all the time in the world."

They had been fishing for nearly an hour before she caught one, a big one. She saw the trout come up out the depths and take it. "Pull on him! Yes, like that!" He slapped the side of his pants. "Bring it in, Rachel, bring your prize in."

And it was a prize, the rainbow trout was the largest she'd ever seen, and looked even more metallic and beautifully colored in the morning sun. She had never felt so elated or triumphant.

"Let's go home now, he said. I don't feel so good."

It was midway back to the cabin when he stopped and gave her his fishing vest, rod, and reel, and said, "They're yours now, everything is yours because you earned it."

That night her grandfather changed his will and left everything to Rachel. And later, in the night, he slipped off and never woke again.

# HIS BOOK

*It was not intended to be a
metaphor for his life*

He found the book he'd written in a bin in the book store marked down to ninety-nine cents.  He had spent five years writing it, about his life in the theater.  Was his life worth only that, less than a dollar now?

The book was the largest in the bin, at 498 pages, and could not be missed with it's bright red color and the gorgeous hand-painted pictures of him when he was twenty back in the Fifties.  He never looked better.

He picked up the book and noticed that the jacket was torn, the inside looked yellowed and faded, and the back was not straight.

Was the book a Voodoo Doll, or was he?

# THE SEXUAL PAIN AND PLEASURES OF LOVE

*Can a man be in love with two women simultaneously?*

It happened on his first day back at work from his honeymoon that Mark fell in love. Absolutely. Completely. Irrevocably. Her name was Denise, and from that day on he thought of her each time he made love to his wife, Charlotte.

Mark's first sighting of Denise was in the copy room at the legal firm of Franklyn Harding & Reynolds where he worked as a paralegal. As the senior paralegal, he worked for the managing partner, and Mark learned later she was hired as one of the legal secretaries for the same partner. She was next in line to use the copier, and he first saw her from behind. She was tall and leggy, with long blonde hair that reached almost to her waist; she resembled one of those sultry women who graced the covers of pulp fiction magazines. She was carrying on a conversation with Josie, another secretary, who was using the copier. They were talking about a TV show they'd seen the night before. Normally Mark would leave and come back later, but not this time. No, this time he would stay and enjoy the view.

"Mark, this is Denice, it's her first day here, and she's going to be a part of your team," said Josie. When Denise turned to face him she seemed younger, the early twenties at most, but her posture and manner made her seem older, worldly, and far removed from her teen years. That impression was reinforced by her outfit: short skirt and sheer top —too sheer for the office? And dark leggings and high heel boots, also questionable. But it was her hands that caught his attention. She was holding several large legal files in her arms and clutching the tops with her long fingers. The way her hands curled over the top of the files with polished fingernails of bright crimson seemed to him as if they were latched on to a lover's back, pulling him closer to her.

"Want to jump ahead of me, Mark? You only have a few pages and mine will take much longer."

Mark didn't say anything, stared at her, and then realized he'd been holding his breath and exhaled slowly, afraid she would notice. "No, go ahead," he said, "no rush, I can wait."

"Did you see Game of Thrones last night," she asked as she began placing documents into the copier.

"Not last night," he said, "but I taped it."

"Best show ever," she said, "I mean it. I tape it and watch it a few times. Living in those times, among those people, that would be something."

"Yes," he replied. "It's so different from our ordinary existence today."

"Exactly. Although I got to see England last year, it was not like that."

Mark had also been to England, after high school and before he started college when he backpacked around the UK with a friend. They hitchhiked mostly, and occasionally rented bicycles to explore the villages of Suffolk east of London. But their most memorable adventures were on the side streets of London, where they walked past Edwardian gabled homes on cobblestoned streets. And it was there in an internet cafe a woman approached them dressed in brightly colored clothes with unkempt hair and wild eyes, grabbed Mark by the arm and spoke urgently to him. "You will marry too soon and fall in love with another," she said. Mark's friend said, "Ignore her; she's crazy."

The woman repeated herself and then said: "You will fall in love with a woman whose name begins with D."

A decade later, standing in the copy room, Mark remembered that prediction. The woman with the crimson nails is named Denise Dalton, and she tells Mark that it's her first real job out of college and she's happy to have landed a job at the firm. *No, I'm the lucky one... So very, very lucky*, thought Mark."

◆ ◆ ◆

Mark and his new bride spent their honeymoon in Bora Bora, where they stayed in an overwater bungalow suspended on stilts over a crystal clear lagoon. They were in the honeymoon section of an isolated resort and saw little of anyone else there. It was clothing optional, and they remained naked most of the time, even while swimming, walking on the beach, or sunbathing themselves nut-brown in the sun. In their nakedness, they talked and learned about their pasts, having met only two months before they married, discussed their future together, their plans for a career, and explored each other's bodies, minds, and dreams.

Charlotte had a very clear vision of her life to come. She wanted three children, a home in the suburbs in a new development, to not work full time after she gave birth to their first child, and to home-school their children —all of which was her experience growing up in Salt Lake City. She was younger than Mark by ten years, but was more set in her ways, and more serious than Mark.

Mark realized on their honeymoon that Charlotte had little time for frivolity, spontaneous, or humor... And that their plans for the future were unlike in most respects, and that they had little in common beyond the music and the movies they both liked. He wanted one child or two at most, and preferred the urban lifestyle, and thought she should remain working even after they started a family together. He was raised in Los Angeles, and that's what he experienced growing up.

Yet their sexual appetite for each other was enormous. They made love constantly, almost from morning coffee to their dinnertime meal, and even afterward until they were exhausted finally. Mark had never experienced that with anyone. He thought he was overly sexual, that she would give out before he did, but she never did. It was the most satisfying feeling he had ever known. The differences in plans for the future? They seemed trivial and unimportant.

In thinking of Denise back at his work station, Mark talked himself out of any real interest in her. He assured himself that she was attractive, no doubt, but so was Charlotte. And the appeal that he felt was just normal male sexual attraction to any sex object, as to a Playboy centerfold. Now that he was married he had his go-to sexual partner, and no need to have sex with anyone else. He prided himself on finding someone who could keep up with him that way. And he loved Charlotte. This was only a harmless flirtation, he told himself, and a bit of sexual tension in the workplace had always been there with others, though he's never dated anyone in the office. Sure, he'd thought about it, but never resorted to it.

Working for the same boss, they often met to discuss certain cases and had working lunches. Once, on an important case where the trial was to begin soon, they sought out a place for a quiet lunch in the green space outside their building. "That looks like a good spot," she said. It was a small picnic table with ferns on either side and leafy tree branches above, away from most foot traffic.

"Sure, that'll do," Mark said, turning and brushing Denise's breast with his arm. The electricity that Mark felt shot through him like a lightning bolt. Later, when Denise was discussing the file, all Mark could do was think about her breasts, what they looked like, how they would feel in his hands; and how much he would love to nibble them with his mouth.

"Mark? Mark, are you listening to me?"

No, he hadn't been. "Sorry, I was thinking about something else just now. Repeat what you said." But as she did his eyes closed and he could picture her breasts again. And he recalled his first sighting of a woman's breast that got him excited when he was ten delivering papers. She was an Asian with enormous dark nipples that were visible through a sheer top.

"Mark, did you get enough sleep last night? You seem to be nodding off."

"Just overworked lately, with the trial coming up in days."

Denise put her hand on his shoulder and said, "If there's anything I can do, just ask."

"I'll let you know if there is," said Mark, and as he did he took her hand in his and said, "I promise."

That night when he and Charlotte made love all he could think about was Denise. He saw her face instead of Charlotte's, her long slim, tanned legs instead of Charlotte's shorter legs... He was grasping Denise's breasts when he pushed himself into Charlotte. And when he grabbed Charlotte by her hair and turned her around, it was Denise's long blonde hair in his hands. He could see her, smell her and feel her there instead of Charlotte.

Later, while Charlotte slept, Mark contemplated what he had experienced. *Is this something I need? Something I must have? Would it ever become a reality?*

He thought about his "first," a girl of 14, like himself at the time, that he met one summer at a birthday party. Her name was Miranda, and when she slow danced with him, she pushed herself into his body so close that he couldn't stop from becoming sexually excited. She felt his erection and instead of pulling away, drew in even closer and kissed his neck.

They danced one more slow dance that way before she asked if he wanted to find some privacy for them. He said he did, and they hunted around until they found a bathroom where he entered her, hard and painful, for both of them. She had young, skinny legs, which he held onto as he thrust into her for no more than a few seconds before he ejaculated.

It had been her "first," she said later. And she added, "It was better than I thought it would be." They met a few more times over the Summer, had sex each time, but she moved before school began. "I love you," she said at their parting, and he said he loved her too. But they never saw each other again, and never tried to. Mark had already started dating someone else by then and felt nothing but relief and shame.

Mark wondered if he could be in love with two women at the same time. Mormons say they can, as he learned when he visited Charlotte's parents in Salt Lake City. They weren't Mormons but knew some in their neighborhood who had multiple wives. And Mark's mother was once a member of commune in the Seventies where she said that went on as well.

She told him about a special broach that she wore and its significance. She said it was a gift from a special friend. He had given it to her when he was about seven. Later, she received other gifts, also from the same friend. And he'd even met the man once when the family was on a beach outing. He was there with his wife and two children which were similar in age to Mark and his brother. When her mother said the man's name, Mark recalled him visiting his house once when he got home from school early. He was tall and thin, like himself, with similar rusty red hair. Later, after his father had died, his mother told him how she and this man had kissed one afternoon at the commune, though nothing more came of it, she said. But Mark always wondered if that was true.

"That one kiss was enough," her mother said, adding, "You can love someone from a distance, sometimes even more strongly than close up."

Mark felt betrayed by her mother's revelation. She had continued to see this man after she was married to his father. And even after his father's death, while the man was married to his own wife. And his grandmother's reaction to the broach told him that she knew there was more to the story than just a kiss. His mother's mother may have been a confidante in the true nature of things, though she never divulged any family secrets.

Denise worked at the firm for only six months before finding a better paying job elsewhere. It was a relief to Mark when he learned she was leaving. The office staff held a short parting celebration with cake at closing, after which most of the staff left. Denise was tidying her work station, putting her personal items in a box, when Mark approached her to say goodbye.

"It's been a joy working with you Mark," she said, I've learned a lot since coming here, and you've taught me a great deal. I hope I haven't been too much of a distraction. You know," pointing to her short skirt, "I'm somewhat of a tease at times, clothing-wise, but I've tried to keep that in check, especially after the office manager got on me for that."

Then she walked over to him and put her arms around him, pressing him towards her, until he could feel her breasts full on him, her hair fragrant against his nose, and the pressure of each of her fingers on his back. She lifted her face and seemed to be unsure about whether to kiss him. She looked back and forth, from eye to eye, contemplating the possibilities. He would have kissed her back. And one kiss would not be enough. But before that moment, he pulled apart. And he drove home.

Charlotte met Mark at the door by holding two glasses of champagne.

"I'm so proud of you," she said and kissed him. "I heard about the case that your firm won that you've been working so hard on. I know you've been distant and distracted, but the case is over now thank goodness. And things will change, won't they?"

Mark pulled Charlotte towards him and gave her a hard, lingering kiss that reminded them both of Bora Bora, of hot, frantic sex, and of passion and pleasure they had not experienced for the last six months.

"Yes, things'll be different, I promise."

# ARE WE ALONE IN THE UNIVERSE?

*This story provides an answer from someone who may know.*

"How can there not be other life forms similar to us?" Said Jeff. "In the news, they said astronomers added another hundred or so planets like our own to their catalog of those that may support life. Hundreds, like our own. Think about that for a minute."

And the two others at the bar with Jeff, his two co-workers, Ernie and Sam, mentally tried to take that in, as best they could after three beers.

"They've cataloged close to 10,000 planets in our own Milky Way galaxy that support life similar to our ours, and expect to find millions, if not billions more in the coming years. *And there are hundreds of billions of galaxies.*"

Ernie and Sam nodded at Jeff, and they all took another sip of their beers.

Jeff stretched tall on his barstool and spoke as loud, pompous and arrogant as if he was lecturing in a college classroom.

"Thus, the question not whether we will be contacted, but why haven't we already been?" He said. "Possible answers? Aliens are waiting for us to reach the nearest star before contacting us. That is the price of membership in the 'galactic club' for other life forms."

All three held their bottles up, clicked them together, and took another sip of their beers.

"How about this: Aliens are so different from us that we cannot ever make contact," Jeff continued. "We are microscopic, even atom-size next to them. Or, we are so gigantic that we cannot sense their minute presence by even our most powerful microscopes. And this: Aliens evolved to a point where their lifeforms exist in a different dimension from ours. That is the ultimate 'galactic club' we must join before contact."

"Excuse the interruption," said a little guy who was just outside the group at the bar. "There is another possibility, one you didn't mention."

Jeff, Ernie, and Sam looked over at him. He was slight of build, thin and angular, and was wearing a heavy overcoat, a hat, and sunglasses, even there at the darkened bar. And he talked as if he was producing each word carefully from a memory device.

"And what in the world would that be?" Said Jeff, not realizing the irony of what he said.

"Maybe aliens have already have made contact... Many years ago, in fact. But maybe they've chosen to treat earthlings like earthlings treat animals in a zoo: visited and viewed, but never interacted with. Well, at least not openly."

That stopped the conversation, and the three, Jeff, Ernie and Sam, looked at one another, and then took another sip of their beers.

Finally, Jeff spoke again. "Well, earthlings are escaping from the zoo, aren't they? We got to the moon and have plans to go to other planets soon."

The little guy eyed the other three with amusement. "Yes, but doesn't it strike you as odd that about the same time as space was conquered that the atom bomb came into being... Something that will send earthlings back to the Stone Age? Was that just coincidence, or purposeful —a stop-gap of sorts?"

There were glassy-eyed looks from Jeff, Ernie, and Sam.

A faint beep came from under the little guy's coat, signaling that his visit to the bar was over. After finishing his beer, he raised the small blue device that he held in his other hand and pressed its button. He was gone, and so were any memories of his appearance there.

# CABIN FEVER AND THE IMPERFECT PARTNER

*Tight quarters can doom the
best of friendships, especially
in Alaska in 1910.*

Jed trudged through the snow cursing every step he took; cursing his bad luck, and his good luck; Alaska, the cold, and most of all, Abe. He could feel his blood receding from his hands and feet, numbing them, a sure sign that it was too cold to be out here. His face would surely follow. There were no sounds but his own movements through the snow, and the faint cracking of ice on the few trees surrounding him.

"I'm leaving," is what Jed had told Abe five days before. "I can't wait for Spring no more."

"It's three hundred miles to Chitina, how you going to do that on your own, without a horse, and in snow higher than you stand without snow shoes? Answer me that, Jed?"

Jed didn't respond, but instead rigged some snowshoes out of the most flexible wood scraps, filled his backpack with enough pemmican for ten days, some powder and lead, rope, and a leather satchel of gold. Then readied his rifle and leather-wrapped Bowie knife.

"Take more if you want," said Abe. "The pemmican or the gold."

"That'll do fine." Jed didn't look at Abe because he couldn't stand looking at him any longer. They had been together for ten years now looking for gold throughout the Wrangell Mountains of Alaska, in the areas north and east of Chitina, wilderness areas that were so remote that others did not go. It was enough, too much, after so many years together.

It was either leave or cut Abe's heart out. His knife in his hand before he started making his snowshoes felt ready to be used for both. It took determination not to plunge it into Abe —almost more than he had left inside him.

Instead, Jed took to work on his snowshoes: splitting the centers of the wood branches, expanded them, nailed them open with cross branches, and attached leather bindings. *They'll do*, he thought.

Jed put on his leather shirt, then his bear coat, and clamped his beaver hat over his head. He picked up his backpack and snow shores.

"You want breakfast first?" Said Abe.

His head down so he wouldn't look at him, Jed said, "Just get out of my way."

"You going by Wilson's Camp? They'll cut you down sure as anything ifn't you're alone."

"I said, get outta my *fuckin'* way!"

Abe stepped aside as if he'd been slapped. Then said, "God be with you, Partner. I'm going to miss you… My friend. We had some times together…"

Jed opened the cabin door and was out before Abe finishing talking. The blowing snow hit his face, and the trek began.

"Good times, and bad times, and everything in between," Abe said to the door. His eyes misted. *Must be the needles of snow,* Abe thought. *It's blowin'* real *good outside.*

Jed reached Wilson's Camp on the sixth day. It was spread across the length and width of the gorge in the big bend part of Wilson's creek. In addition to the cabins, there was a high wall now and no way to get beyond except through the gate. The payment was usually half the gold you had if you were lucky. If not, they'd slice your throat and take everything else.

From where Jed hunkered down in the deep powder above, he could hear dogs yapping and the sounds of horses in the barn areas. Smoke rising from chimneys hung low and gave the camp a hazy, unreal look. Because of the snow and cold, few men ventured out. When they did, he saw they were armed with pistols and knives.

Was there a way he could get over the wall and not be noticed? He tried approaching twice at night and heard snarling dogs barking before he got ten feet from the wall. He'd be caught, for sure. He tried burrowing under the snow, but found that the gate was too close to the ground. The gorge was too steep to climb, even without the snow. All he could do was wait and hope some plan might come to him.

It had been a week since he got to Wilson's Camp and he still couldn't think of a way to get beyond it and continue his trek. Reclining on his side, he had done nothing but look out over the wide-stretching landscape, and eat his pemmican —dried meat, fat, and berries mushed together into frozen patties— and he had run out of it now.

There was no game near the camp, nor any way to get any without firing a shot and alerting someone. And he could smell whiffs of broiled meat, probably elk or moose, from the camp below, and that made him more hungry.

It was getting colder, colder than he'd ever experienced before. He couldn't risk a fire so close to the camp. He had to do something. Or die there. He knew from his many years in the mountains that he was only a few days away from death. He had no food, and he hadn't been able to feel his feet for days.

He cursed Abe for having to leave when he did. *It was your fault, Abe!* And Jed knew if he went back, he'd kill Abe for sure. *You made me leave, and you'll die when I get back!*

Jed got to his feet, put on his snowshoes, and started back. And he cursed Abe with every step he took. *I ain't spending another minute with you. Not one minute! You're going to die for sure… For sure!*

Abe had been loutish, coarse, and crude—worse each year, and now was a completely degenerate animal. A filthy pig beyond words or description. Jed had put up with it for too long.

Each morning began with the same routine. Abe would rise and stretch, popping his shoulders and fingers. And then he'd piss in the pot, always missing most of it. After that he'd growl within his chest, raise a big glob of phlegm and aim it at the pot, missing most times as well. His soiled union suit showed where he'd missed. He was a hairy man, and some hairs protruded through the fabric, coarse hairs, some gray, particularly around the crotch. Tobacco spit stains on his chest were darker than the piss stains below. And his entire union suit was hard with his sweat as well and gave off an odor even worse than the piss.

Nights were worst of all. Abe would think of the whores he'd had —his favorites, Nellie and Yolanda in Chitina, Mindi and Pearl in

Valdez— and call out their names, say what he'd like to do with them, take his cock out and whip it for hours until he'd cum or was spent. And that stunk more than anything.

Ninety-five days Jed has spent in the small cabin with Abe, longer than any man could endure. On the Ninety-sixth day, he left.

Now it was a choice between survival and death. He had avoided the ferocious wolf packs, but could not see how to avoid the human demons of Wilson's Camp if he ventured there. At least a wolf attack would be a quick death, pulled down and remorselessly eaten. While the latter might take hours, and done with relish and glee. Better to return.

This was the first winter Jed and Abe spent together. They'd been caught by an early snow storm in September and had to quickly build a small cabin after their way out of the canyon was made impassable by horseback. Looking at the sky they could tell more was coming fast; all the signs were there of a long and terrible winter.

They hunkered down and waited for Spring.

This had been their best year prospecting for gold, which usually lasted from mid-June to early September, and they stayed too long because they were too successful. It had been Jed's idea to go further this year because their last two years they'd found barely enough gold to sustain them over the winter. The easy pickings were gone, and they had to go further and higher to get to where the newcomers wouldn't go. That's how they got snowbound at eight thousand feet, in the meanest and heartless part of the Wrangell Mountains.

Winters were usually spent in Valdez, or Kattala where Jed had a wife for five years, a pretty Russian named Misha who he met just after she arrived. But the first year he returned without much gold, she found someone else. Abe had also been married for awhile, to an Aleut named Birdsong, but that ended after only one year. When Jed asked why Abe said "Don't ever say anything about her again… Ever!

For the first couple of months, they were able to find deer and beaver in the canyon, but that ended, and they had to start on the horses. Jed's horse Emily was the last to go and Jed got sick to his stomach when taking her down.

Jed and Abe first met when they were part of a survey party exploring the Nome territory in the northern part of Alaska. They were both from West Texas and knew some of the same people around Midland and Odessa. When the survey ended, they struck out on their own to become prospectors.

Being with Abe wasn't a problem during the Summer months prospecting for gold. They exchanged a few words during the day, but neither was much of a talker, and both liked it that way. And in the evenings, after they'd eaten, there was an unspoken rule that they didn't talk after they went to bed. Too intimate. And they bedded down far enough away from each other that it wasn't a problem.

The final straw for Jed was when Abe tumbled out of bed while whacking himself and calling out the name of Mindi, his favorite whore in Valdez.

"Can't you keep it down, I'm five feet away from you, not across the canyon," said Jed.

Abe looked at Jed astounded. He had broken protocol and spoke. Abe was seething.

"Fuck you! You don't have to be holed up with me, Jed, you can leave any time you want."

Jed said nothing for awhile and just looked at Abe.

"I'm sorry for sayin' that. Just forget it," said Jed finally.

Abe was still seething. "You could leave anytime. We could square up tonight if you want."

"It's a cold one tonight," said Jed. "Too cold for anything." The next morning was when Jed left.

◆ ◆ ◆

It had taken six days to get to Wilson's Camp, but that was with food and before he lost feeling in his legs. Jed didn't know if he could make it back.

Was it the fifth day on the return now? Or was it the sixth? Jed didn't recall. Most of the time, his head was filled with memories of other places, and other times; growing up on a ranch, his aunt and uncle that raising him when his parents were killed by Indians. He sang songs that he learned from his aunt and repeated bawdy poems that he got from his uncle. He cursed Abe for being like he was; and cursing himself for walking out when he did.

Jed was stumbling, staggering and lurching from tree to tree on legs that no longer responded to him. They were like wooden logs on which he teetered. He tried not to think about that or look down. He only focused on what was ahead of him —at the pure white of the snow that blended with the grayish white of the sky. It hadn't snowed since he left over two weeks before. Too cold, no doubt. And he was able to follow his tracks back.

He'd left his backpack at the Wilson's Camp, gold and all. Survival was first; everything else didn't matter. He dropped his rifle on his third day. Too heavy. He even dropped his knife. No need for it. If the wolves found him, what good would it do to try to hold them off. A quick death would be welcomed.

He scooped up some snow every hour, to keep himself from getting thirsty. His only food was on the third day back when he found a snow hare frozen near a tree. He pulled it apart and ate it raw over the next day.

In his mind, he could see the cabin again and Abe. And he could see that Abe had shaved, bathed, put on clean clothes, and had prepared a meal for him —elk stew, his favorite. There was a fire going in the cabin, and it was warm there. Abe was smiling at him and saying, "I thought you could make it back, and you did. And that's why I cleaned up... Just for you, Partner!"

But Jed didn't make it back. He collapsed within sight of the cabin and couldn't go any further. His last view of life was of the smoke rising from the chimney, and his last thought, when he knew his last moment had arrived, was of saying to Abe, *I didn't mean what I said to you, Partner. Bad habits or not, whether you piss poorly and miss the pot, jack off till you drop, or do anything a man does cause he is a man, you are my best friend, and always will be!*

# THE EXCHANGE

*Dialogue during a drug buy
can include profanity, hostility,
danger, and be a public service.*

As Clyde looked toward the entrance for the third time, a hand tapped him lightly on his right shoulder. "Don't say nuthin', just keep staring out that way. Stay cool, act like you're waitin' for someone and he ain't here yet. And then turn back slow… Look down and drink your coffee all calm like."

"What the fuck you talkin' about, Frisco? You're late, *you're always late.*" Clyde said, as he turned and looked straight at Frisco who was clearly uncomfortable with that.

Clyde said that so loud all the people in Rudy's Deli could hear him, yet only the waitress looked over at the two men sitting in adjacent booths in the far corner of the deli.

"Nobody knows you here, man, that's why I picked this place," said Clyde. "And why you sittin' in that booth on the opposite side? Is that some weird James *fuckin'* Bond shit? How you gonna to pass me the stuff from there?"

Frisco looked down with his eyes and softly said, "I got it here under my shirt."

Well, it ain't my hand, *mutherfuck*, and that's where it should be!"

"It'll be there soon. Now turn around and just be looking," said Frisco.

"Turn around?" Said Clyde. "Why you doin' all dis weird shit?

"We've got eyes on us," said Frisco. "Guy over in the corner, blue shirt. And another, maybe, at the counter, leather jacket... *No, don't look! Jeez!*"

Frisco breathed hard and hunched his back, what he did when he was angry. *What a fuckin' turd. Last time I do this with him.* Then he said, "I'm gonna leave it in the john, under the sink."

"Like hell you are! Ain't no police here, just regulars, like me."

"The guy in the corner, with the blue shirt, he's got a bulge on his leg like it's a piece, a big one. And leather jacket, on this kinda day? That'll hide a piece. You savvy? No, don't look again... OK, just slow like. Look at the door, and half at 'em."

"So they ain't no regulars. So what? Don't make 'em cops. And how am I goin' to test it? I always do, don't I?"

"When you goin' to trust me? How long we been doin' this? Two months now? And you know where I hang, so what's the fuckin' problem?

"No problem. Just routine. Always."

Frisco shook his head. "I'm gettin' up now, and go to the john, leavin' it under the sink. And when I come out, you go to the john. I'll go to where you sittin' and feel somethin' under the cushion, the money. Got it?"

"Yeah, but it ain't necessary."

"Just do it!" Said Frisco. I'll order somethin' and eat it. You climb out the window. Understand? You don't come out of the john. The guys with bulges on their ankles, blue shirt, and leather jacket, they're gonna wait 'til they figure the buy's been made. They'll be watchin' for you. I'll take my sweet time eatin'. Maybe get some pie, maybe not. When I absolutely, positively know you're gone, I leave, out the front door."

Clyde turned toward Frisco. "This ain't happenin' lessen I test it first."

Frisco looked at Clyde, shook his head, turned it to one side, and said, "Man, why you wanna fuck this up? I said we gotta do it like I said."

"It ain't happening' that way." Clyde lifts up his right leg and plops it on the table. "See my shoes?"

"What? What you talkin' about?"

My shoes, *nigga*, what am I *fuckin'* wearing?"

"Them's cheap ass Hong Kong Air Jordans you got outta South Street."

"No, they's the real thing. Cost three-eighty at the Nike store, I get 'em for two hundred. They Nike Air Jordans, *"Just Do It"* Air Jordans."

Then Clyde leaned forward at Frisco and opened his eyes so wide they nearly popped out. "Just do it, *just do it!*"

Frisco shook his head again, slower this time. "OK, but this is the last time, mutherfucker... No more after this!" He got up, took a plastic bag from under his Oakland Raiders jersey, and gave it to Clyde. Clyde tested the white powder it contained and handed a packet of money to Frisco.

Within seconds of the exchange, two men, one wearing a blue shirt and the other a leather jacket, were upon Frisco and Clyde and handcuffed them. And within seconds three other men entered, guns drawn.

Frisco and Clyde were on the ground now, two feet apart, as the man with the blue shirt was counting the money, while the one in the leather jacket was tagging the white powder in the plastic bag. "Do it like I told you, and this wouldn't have happened, never would've happened,' said Frisco, muttering softly.

"Yeah, my bad, it's on me," said Clyde.

What Clyde didn't say, but thought, was this: *No, it is all yours, all yours for what you did to my brother Mikey. And you're a three-time loser, mandatory life, so it's* vaya con Dios *mutherfucker! And after I testify, I can start a new life somewhere else,* as the DA promised. *Mikey always wanted me to quit, and now I'm gonna.*

# RETURN TO ROCA VERDE

*A short story that is part
fact and part reverie.*

To talk about where I was born is not easy for me. I have been there only once that I can recall, three years ago, when I returned to my birthplace at the age of 52. Yet when I reached the place I had heard so much about, from so many different people, I turned away from it, literally, and returned home. I don't know exactly why I did that. But I wish to write about that experience to understand it if I can.

When I first heard about my birthplace, Roca Verde, in the State of Durango, Mexico, I was four. My father told me it was 'filled with beauty.' He said that it was green, it had a creek, and it always had water flowing between the craggy rocks surrounding the village. That description was followed by another, later that day, from my mother who called it, "the most depressing place on earth."

It was then that I decided I would learn everything I could about Roca Verde before going there myself. I talked to my father and mother about the place, and my older brother Carlos, who was seven when the family left there. I also asked others —uncles, aunts, cousins, and others who were from there to tell me about the place.

An odd thing happened in my twenties: I began telling people who asked all about my birthplace as if I'd been there. To some extent, that was true, I had been there, often, through the descriptions of others. And I carried those proxy memories inside of me where they were contributed to, enhanced, and made different by additional layers, until they became transformed and mine: as a butterfly might emerging from a cocoon.

My parents, Margarita and Jose, were probably the most mismatched couple on earth. He was tall at six feet three inches, and a brawny 250 pounds; she diminutive at just five feet and never weighed more than 100 pounds. His skin color was a deep bronze, and he had dark, almost jet black hair and eyes; she had pale skin that was flawless, and hair the color of copper.

And in temperament, they were almost complete opposites: he quiet, soft-spoken, a loner, and seldom reflective of anything; she talkative, gregarious, energetic and the center of any conversation. But what they shared was that they were both beautiful people. He was handsome with a jutting jaw and dimples, and she was gorgeous with green eyes that shined.

They must have come together sexually because they had five children, but how they did that was a mystery to virtually anyone who knew them. When they were together they argued, about *everything*. To call them incompatible and their relationship loveless is an understatement. There was attraction, but a relationship that was tense, painful, difficult, suffocating, dreadful, and ultimately unbearable for both.

They were both ambitious, each in their own way. But how they would achieve their aims in life differed greatly. Similarly, their likes and dislikes for common things like what they ate and what they did for fun were vastly different. So too their feelings toward family and obligations. Ultimately, they could not be united nor raise a family together.

Of course, I didn't know everything that happened between them when I was younger, yet even then I could sense that they should never have married. Both my parents were reticent about talking to the children about their feelings toward the other. Only two facts were known for certain: they separated immediately after the birth of their first child, and periodically came together briefly for a few days to have four other children.

I once read a book called *Death and Dishonor on the Oregon Trail*. It was on a required reading list in one of my classes in high school. It tells of a couple who make the arduous trek to the Oregon Territory in the 1850s in a wagon train; a man and a woman who met and married before they began the difficult journey just so they could go there; bound in a loveless relationship that grows even less so with each day until the final, very depressing end.

The similarity to my parents was not lost on me. And this passage in particular seemed apt:

"The day's hardships hid the hatred that they felt for one another, and kept it in check while they dealt with more pressing daily problems like snakes, all manner of diseases, cuts and gashes, hunger, obsessive heat and bitter cold."

The author of the book, Paul Gross, peeled back the allure and adventure of the pioneers in his novel, and allowed the reader to see how life existed. He captured the daily tragedy of living with someone you hate, and hates you in return, that sometimes things don't improve over time, better than anyone I've ever read. He lays out the problem of finding lust and love outside of marriage in a series of brilliant scenes: the man's late-night wandering and his tragic longing for an older prostitute; and the woman's shocking sexual encounters with dozens of other men in the wagon train.

When I read Gross's novel it turned my stomach, as well as turning off any desire for marriage, travel or even adulthood —at least for a while. Few books have done that to me. It was like a virus, contagious upon contact, invading my mind and making me ill with a fever, showing everyday, familiar things can be the horror of life, and that a happy ending to everything isn't always possible. The truth of life is that unhappiness is the norm, and happiness is unattainable except in short, unsustainable moments.

While my father never talked about my mother in any way, good or bad, he did frequently mention Roca Verde. it was where he was born, and where his mother still lived back then. And when he mentioned it, he always attached a word to it: *bonito* Roca Verde, *lindo* Roca Verde, or h*ermoso* Roca Verde, the way a man would talk about someone they loved —beautiful, lovely, and gorgeous. And sometimes when he mentioned Roca Verde he would open his eyes wide and look out, far away, as if into memories. His present surroundings meant little to him; he was too deeply immersed in his vision… In utter love of it. And he would sometimes stay that way for awhile, and then come back to the present.

While my father talked about Roca Verde often, my mother seldom did, as if it was best forgotten. About the only thing I recall her saying about it was once when she said "I got sick there and almost died, and that made things clear for me about where I wanted to be and where I shouldn't be."

What prompted me to go to Roca Verde when I did was that I had closed a chapter in my life. I had sold my business and was indecisive about what to do next. I looked at my life with a little more objectivity and contemplation. I was in a transition point in my life, with no immediate obligations or ties to time or place. And if I had a "bucket list," a visit to Roca Verde would be in the single digit hierarchy. And, somewhat sad for me, I had always looked forward towards the greater part of my life. Now I had the sensation of feeling that the greater part was behind me, that life had become finite, and the number of birthdays to come was becoming smaller.

I remember sitting in a chair listening to a financial advisor about what to do with a sum of money I was to receive shortly. He mentioned that his aim was to see to it that it would last me for the next twenty six years or so, the number of years still remaining for me based on an actuarial table. I remember thinking, *Is that all I have?* It was a strange felling, as if I had been given a calendar and I was to mark off each day now in a countdown to the end. Counting the days down to what? I felt a loss, something was at an end, and I sensed the preciousness of existence, of less time to be consumed, experienced, enjoyed.

Later, meeting friends at a bar, I felt melancholy and anxious. Happy Hour was a sad hour, with the sun's setting symbolic of the coming of darkness. The sun that set that day had been robust and arrogant, but disappeared too early in clouds that had formed on the horizon... In my mind, and in fact.

I talked to my wife later and her counsel was a perfect balance of positive and negative reinforcements, between gentleness and violence to each point I made about the trip. I knew no one there now, and no real places to visit. The place had, at one time, about twenty residents, but I didn't know if it was even inhabited now. It was one of the most remote places in Mexico, "off the grid" as it gets even for there, built long ago on a cliff side.

There were no roads accessing it, only a steep foot path up cliff that took several hours to climb. A donkey or possibly a jeep would be used to get to the where the path began. Prior to that would be a train trip of half a day to Presidios, and two flights before then, Los Angeles to Mexico City, and then to Durango. It was a journey that would take three days there and three days back.

In the end, I decided to do it alone. It was my journey. I would hire a guide in Presidios and that would be enough.

About two weeks later I was in the tourism offices of El Oro, on the plaza in Presidios speaking to the ex-mayor, Eduardo Jimenez. He spoke some English, which was better than my Spanish and we got along quite well. He recommended a cousin of his, Esteban, that would make the journey with me, along with his friend, Chino, as a precaution. We would depart at sunrise, take almost five hours to get there, and return the same day.

Did anyone still live in Roca Verde? Jimenez didn't know of anyone. Maybe someone did, but there had been no contact with anyone in Presidios, the closest town, for years. If the path was still OK, Esteban would get me to Roca Verde, I was assured. He was the best.

Determination is a fine thing in principal, but can waver in the hot sun of Mexico high in the rugged terrain of Durango. And I was not young or energetic anymore, nor obviously older and wiser, otherwise I would have not made the journey. But my youthful dreams of returning to my birthplace were about to become reality finally.

The jeep took us only half-way there, with the last part, almost four hours in the hot sun —not one as I thought— the crucible. And I was accompanied by only Esteban, Chino would remain with the jeep.

Feeling a little like Pizarro the Spanish conquistador leading his men up the Andes in Peru, Esteban and I slowly made the ascent. The path had not used in years and at times disappeared altogether, but we kept moving onward with Esteban's ability and sense of direction. Esteban spoke often to me. He was a real talker, but didn't speak much English. Thus, he carried on and I understood, at best, every other word, mostly when he would use English words.

I learned that Esteban was part Indian and had three sons, one of whom had died recently. Another was in the Army, and the third did guide work as he did, but was on his honeymoon. Esteban seemed like a kind and decent family man, leading a simple life. And he appeared to feel genuine sorrow that his son wasn't available for this trip. Chino wasn't half the guide that his son was, he told me.

"*Alli*," said Esteban, quite a few times, and pointed to our destination when I seemed to be lagging. "We're almost there."

Squinting upwards and nodding at him, I would acknowledge what he said. It was so hot and dusty that my only thought was to wonder if there was shade there.

"*Si, si, alli, alli.*" said Esteban. "*Alli!*"

I pretended I didn't hear him towards the end. The heat so pressed on my lungs that I could not inhale enough air to answer. I couldn't recall ever being this hot. I wondered why Esteban wasn't bothered by the heat. Did he feel it at all? I closed my eyes and thought of what I wanted most in the all the world then: an ice cold Screwdriver sipped poolside was what this middle-aged guy wanted most in the world at that moment.

Finally, we reached the elevation of Roca Verde. Even before it was in sight I felt its presence. As the first structures appeared, re-cessed back, no more than fifty feet away from us, I stopped, and put up my arm to signal Esteban to stop. There were about a dozen structures, most in ruins, and they seemed deserted. They were the kind made of rocks from the surroundings, and high mud walls connecting some of them.

And there were flies, hordes of them, that appeared as we stood there. They were bigger than what I was used to, buzzing around, grayish, tenacious and annoying.

I yelled, *Hola*! Nothing.

I did that several times, louder each time. A faint echo came back at me. Nothing else.

Esteban was watching me, waiting.

I breathed deeply, turned, and started the long trek back. Why? I didn't want to change what either my father or my mother said about Roca Verde.

From a distance Roca Verde seemed ordinary, without character or uniqueness, but to them it was vastly different. He had loved it, and she was repulsed by it. I turned and chose to keep both versions intact.

When I returned home my wife didn't ask why I never entered Roca Verde. I think she knew just by looking at my face and seeing all the feelings displayed there, a battleground of desperate warring emotions, memories, wishes and regrets, that it would be unwise to add more.

# MY LIFE IN PICTURES

*Can a person's wish after a lifetime
be captured in just one word?*

My furnished apartment in Shady Oaks, the senior living facility I just moved into is perfect for me. The other place was getting too expensive. This one fits my budget, though it is far from the city. No friends left to visit, so that's not a problem.

I didn't bring much because I don't have much these days. The closet was twice as large as I needed for my clothes, and I only needed two drawers for the rest of my things instead of the six that the chest of drawers provided. The bed is smaller than I'm used to, and that's fine with me. The mattress is softer and more comfortable than my other one, and the bed sits lower, which is a plus these days. I won't need a step stool now, and I won't fear to fall off.

I have quite a lot of framed pictures and put some of those on the dresser and the small bedside table. The bigger ones will grace the walls.

This is the last place I will live, I know that, and want to make sure that I am surrounded by everything and everyone I loved in my life. Of course, pictures from my Army service are here, with all my platoon buddies. They're all gone now, except for me.

Most of the pictures are of my children and their families: all my kids, even those who don't call me now. Kids are cute when they're growing up, and, later, not so much.

I put pictures of my two wives up. I don't know why I did that. Maybe it's because I don't care to hold grudges any longer. I haven't talked to them in decades —don't even know where they are, or even if they're still alive. Funny, but I still feel something for them. Love? Hate? Perhaps a bit of both.

Sitting on my bed, I can see my whole life in pictures. God, I wish there was some way to tell those people… Sorry.

# ESTATE SALE AD

*Ernest Hemingway's 6-word story*
*—For sale: baby shoes, never worn*
*— Updated for the computer age.*

*Estate Sale at* **9765 Eucalyptus Drive West in Newbury Park, California. Cash or check only. One family's entire household possessions. A five-bedroom home in which two adults and four children lived. The items are available for pickup only. Bids accepted beginning October 1, the day on which police release the residence from hold as a crime scene. Some damage from gunshots. Also, blood splatters may be present on items though every effort was made by a professional cleanup crew to remove. All funds to be donated to charity by surviving grandparents who have left the country. All Sales Final; items are "As-Is."**

# WOULD SHE BE MY FIRST?

*A question for the narrator,
as well as for the reader.*

Should I go and see what the problem is? No, my father always said to keep out of there.

*There it is again, another scream… Much louder this time. Shit, I must go. Dammit!*

I locked the front door of the small store and raced out the back and up the stairs to the rooms above the store.

*Damn, I forgot the passkey.* I didn't need it since the door to the room where I heard the scream again was wide open —as were the man's pants with an enormously engorged penis held in the hand of an equally enormous man who was almost twice my size. He was on top of a young girl who was even smaller than me, and I was small for my age then, at 110 pounds.

"Eres grande para mi… Muy grande… Muy grande!" *You're too big for me… Too big… Too big!* She said in Spanish.

"Get off her," I said. And then, when he didn't even turn around, I yelled, "Get the fuck off her or I'll call the police… La Policia!"

This time he stopped, turned around slowly and looked at me from head to toe. I was twelve but looked even younger. He was a huge, broad-shouldered man with black, unkempt hair and olive skin tanned darker by the sun. He could have easily flicked me aside if I tried to intervene, but probably thought it was best to leave since I had mentioned the police. And even if he didn't understand English, saying "La Policia" was all the Spanish I needed to use.

I wanted the police there less than he did probably, but he didn't know that. Because they wouldn't look kindly on learning a preteen was renting rooms out by the hour to what he knew were prostitutes.

The huge man looked down at the girl and said, "Pinche puta." *Fucking whore.* And then let out a stream of other loud profanities in Spanish as he got off the bed, did up his fly and left the room.

I looked at the girl more closely and noticed that she seemed much older than before, maybe mid-thirties or even forty.

"Gracias," she said, "muchas gracias." *Thank you, thank you very much,* she said in Spanish.

"Para nada." *For nothing at all.*

She had pulled down her skirt over her legs when the man climbed down from her, but her top was still off, and she was naked from the waist up. She had enormous breasts, long, reddish brown hair, and her bronze skin glistened in the light of a table lamp.

I reached for a sheet that had fallen on the floor and handed it to her. Instead of wrapping herself with it, she crunched it up, placed it behind her, and sat up. Then she patted the bed in front of her and invited me to sit next to her. I hesitated and then did so shyly, trying not to stare at her chest.

Her lipstick was smeared, and her mascara was smudged, but she still looked alluring. There was the faint scent of body odor in the air, but mostly I smelled perfume —strong flowery perfume, like all the samples at Sears.

"You're Yolanda?"

"Si," she said, "Yolanda."

"My name is Jorge… George."

She took my hand and put it on her left leg. Then she slowly moved it up and down her thigh. Her touch was arousing, and she noticed.

Nothing more was said or done for a very long time.

I looked at her, and I could sense what she was thinking. Because it was the same thing I was thinking. *He's never done it before…. And it would be a reward for him… Because of what he did for me.*

I closed my eyes, hoping that not seeing her would sway me from what I wanted to do next. It didn't work. Upon opening my eyes, she made the situation even worse by taking off her skirt, tossing it aside, and became entirely naked.

My thoughts went to the numerous times I had seen her climb those steps with other men, maybe dozens of times over the last few weeks. She was the prettiest of them, the one most popular with the men.

As was the routine, she would leave five dollars in the cigar box by the door after her short stay in the room of perhaps half an hour or less. I could hear the footsteps, and would retrieve the money —but also occasionally steal a glance of her legs, her backside, and her hair swaying back and forth as she walked away in impossibly tall high heels.

And as she walked away sometimes, I would imagine….

I'm sure she knew what I was thinking, that I was trying to decide if she should be the first for me, that I was weighing all the pros and cons. She would wait until I decided, wait for as long as I needed to decide.

Would she be my first?

# ABOUT THE AUTHOR

## John Corral

An award-winning author of mysteries, thrillers, suspense, legal dramas, and westerns, he also co-wrote and edited women's stories of love and life with Tanya Angel, and contributed and edited poetry with Ian Lewis and Iris Mede.

Books by the author include SERIAL SINS OF SIBERIA, LUST, LIES, AND LOVE, GETTING SADDAM'S GOLD, LOVE TIMES ELEVEN, THE GRISLY EFFECTS OF GREEN, DID HOLLYWOOD CAUSE THE CUBAN MISSILE CRISIS?, HIS FINAL RESTING PLACE: ELVIS, REDHEADS ARE RELENTLESS, DELPHINA: VOODOO QUEEN, 30 FLASHES OF FICTION, 15 FLASHES OF FICTION, 15 MORE FLASHES OF FICTION, MYSTERY AND MALICE, IMPERFECT KILLING, PROSECUTION MISCONDUCT, REMEMBERING DIXIE, BEYOND THERE BE DRAGONS and THE MOST DANGEROUS MAN IN THE WORLD.

Books with Tanya Angel include THE SECRET LIVES OF SMILES, THE DUCHESS, WHERE THE HEART IS, and WHEN THE HEART LAUGHS IT SHOW AND WHEN IT DOESN'T IT SHOWS EVEN MORE.

Books with Ian Lewis and Iris Mede include FLOWING LIQUID LIFE, DREAMS OF A PERPETUAL DREAMER, EVOLVING LOVE, LET

LOVE FLOAT, ORDINARY LIVES EXTRAORDINARY LOVES, LET LOVE LEAD THE WAY, REAL PASSIONS REAL LOVE, LOVE THAT CHANGES EVERYTHING, THE SENSE OF SORROWS PAST, LOVE DEVILISH LOVE DIVINE, TALKING DIRTY ABOUT DESIRE, LOVE WORTH REMEMBERING, THE PLEASURES AND PAIN OF LOVE, WHEN LOVE LIFTS YOU HIGH, and WHEN LOVE SIZZLES.

John is also the author of TWO BROTHERS, a western, 3 LIFE LES-SONS, an essay, and SEEING YOU, a book of poetry.